Mara
plants a Seed

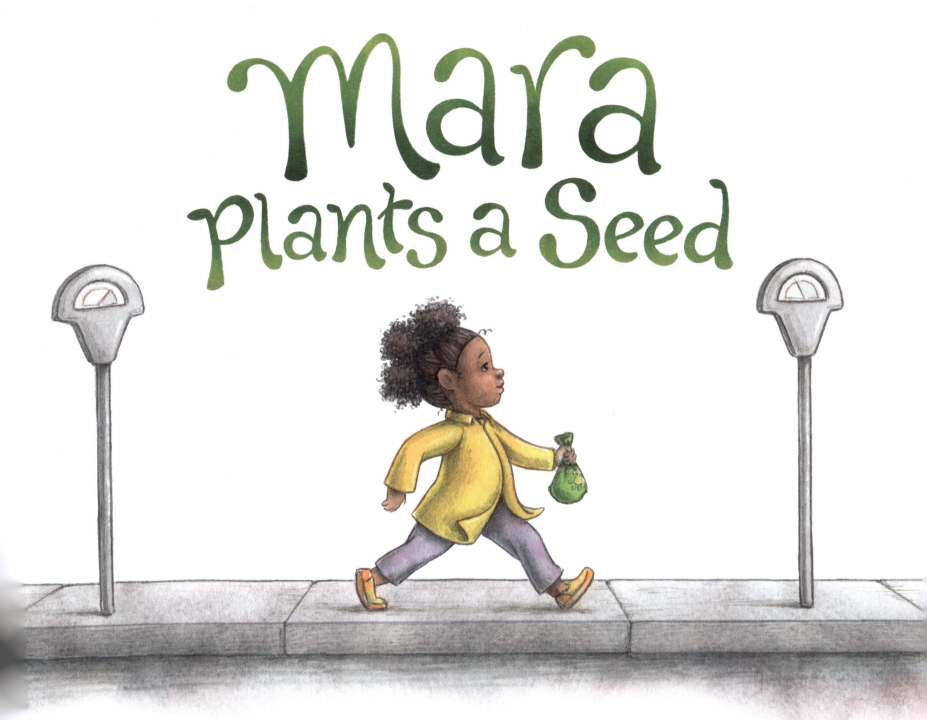

Robert Furrow and **Donna Jo Napoli**

Illustrated by **Melissa Bailey**

Science, Naturally!
An imprint of Platypus Media, LLC
Washington, D.C.

Mara Plants a Seed

Hardcover first edition • April 2025 • ISBN: 978-1-958629-76-5
Paperback first edition • September 2025 • ISBN: 978-1-958629-86-4
eBook first edition • April 2025 • ISBN: 978-1-958629-77-2

Written by Robert Furrow and Donna Jo Napoli, Text © 2025
Illustrated by Melissa Bailey, Illustrations © 2025

Project Manager, Cover and Book Design: Violet Antonick, Washington, D.C.
Senior Editor: Caitlin Burnham, Washington, D.C.
Editors: Hannah Thelen, Washington, D.C.
           Skyler Kaczmarczyk, Washington, D.C.
Editorial Assistants: Sudeeksha Dasari and Gweneth Kozlowski

Spanish edition coming soon.

Teacher's Guide available at the Educational Resources page of ScienceNaturally.com.

Published by:
Science, Naturally! - An imprint of Platypus Media, LLC
   750 First Street NE, Suite 700
   Washington, DC 20002
   202-465-4798
   Info@ScienceNaturally.com • ScienceNaturally.com

Library of Congress Control Number: 2024947700

10 9 8 7 6 5 4 3 2 1

The empty lot
belonged
to no one.

Mara thought it looked tired
and sad.

Crushed water bottles,

crinkled wrappers,

broken toys,
into the trash can.
"Easy!"

But now the lot looked empty.

Mara planted
50 sunflower seeds.

The wind whistled.
Seeds rolled.

The rain whooshed and ran in gullies.
Seeds washed away.

Only a few lucky sunflower seeds remained

under the earth,
where no one could see,

not even Mara.

Mara visited every day

just to check.

When would her sunflowers come?

The sun came out
and so did other visitors.

One brought an apple core.

Another buried bones.

Two more
scattered worms.

The apple core turned to soil.
The bones decayed.
The worms dug tunnels.

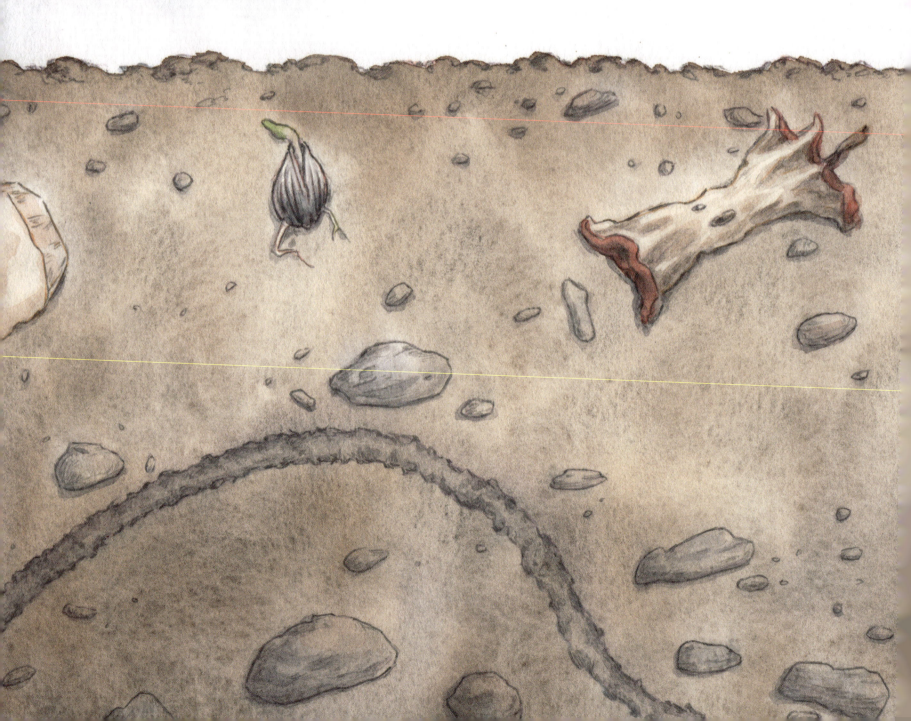

The earth grew rich
and airy
and ready.

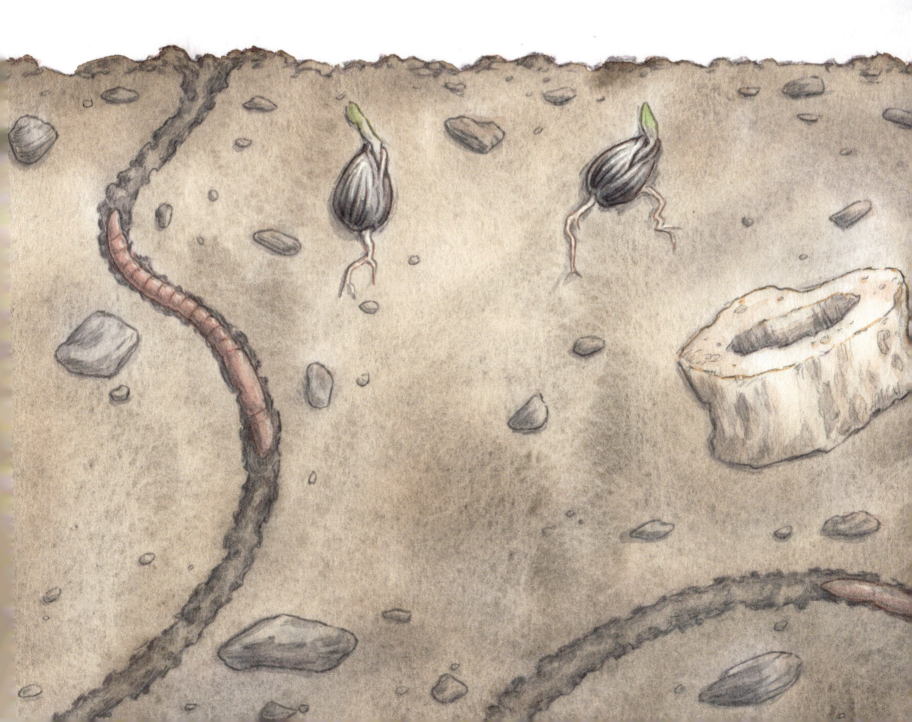

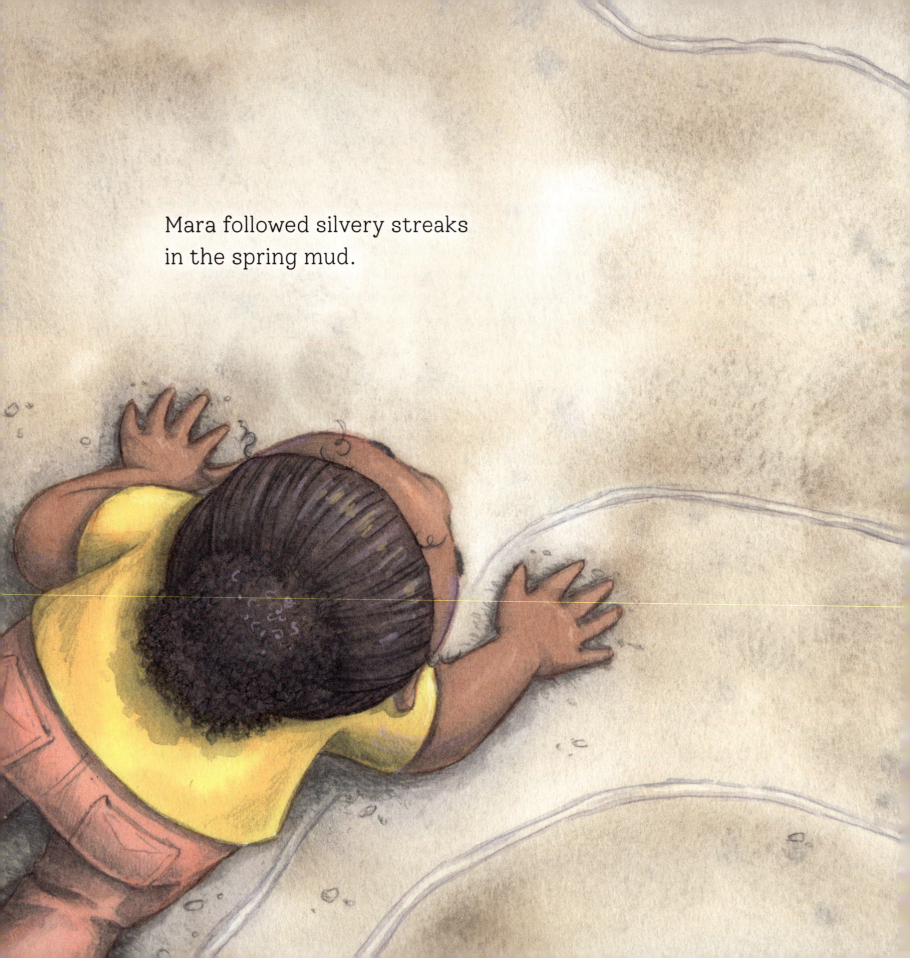

Mara followed silvery streaks
in the spring mud.

Did her seeds feel Mara walking?
Did they feel the snails sliding?

More visitors came.

Messy ones sneezed coneflower seeds.

Busy ones carried violet seeds.

Noisy ones spit
watermelon seeds.

Stubby sprouts peeked up here

and here

and here.

Mara followed rambly paths
in the summer dirt.

Are those my sunflowers?

Those?

Those?

Even more visitors came
to explore among
the newly lanky sprouts.

Some nibbled weeds.

Some ate insects.

And one dumped her fishbowl water.

Mara followed giant footprints,
stepping neatly inside them
to weave through green stalks.

Snakes slithered under watermelon vines,
bees sampled violets,
butterflies drank from poppies,
all beneath the watchful eyes of birds.

Where was her yellow?

"Aha!
A sunflower,
only one from all those seeds.
But so many surprises."

Mara laughed.

"Look at the yellows
and oranges,
the pinks
and purples,
and so many shades of green!
What happened in this garden?"

A mystery,
a quiet, generous secret
created by so many,
kept by the earth,
savored by all.

She sat down in the middle
and breathed deep
of the sweet scents.

The garden rustled and buzzed.

**To Mara and Neve, with love
from Daddy and Nonna.**

– R.F. & D.J.N.–

To all the gardeners in my life.

– Melissa Bailey –

Flowering plants grow from seeds.

Inside a seed are food and the blueprints to build a complete plant. But seeds cannot grow without help from their environment.

Water, light, and temperature tell the seed that it's time to sprout. Soil has nutrients for the growing plant to use. Sunlight and air allow the plant to extend upwards and outwards.

When all of these things work together, a seed will sprout and grow into a new plant. Insects, birds, and other animals may loosen the soil, add nutrients, pollinate, and help in many other ways.

You can plant seeds and watch your garden grow just like Mara!

Robert Furrow is a gardener, an educator, a birder, and a parent. He teaches many shades of introductory biology, including wildlife natural history and how to garden for wildlife habitat. He currently lives in Davis, California.

Contact: Robert.Furrow@ScienceNaturally.com

Donna Jo Napoli has published books for preschoolers through high schoolers. She is a mother, a grandmother, a gardener, a dancer, a professor, and a dual citizen of Italy and America, currently living in Swarthmore, Pennsylvania.

This is her sixth book co-authored with her son, Robert Furrow.

Contact: Donna.Jo.Napoli@ScienceNaturally.com

Melissa Bailey is the daughter of an avid gardener and granddaughter of a farmer. She is also an award-winning illustrator of 50+ children's books and the author/illustrator of two picture books. Melissa loves living in rural Michigan, somewhere in between Flint and Detroit, thinks it would be awesome to live in a treehouse, and tries to remember to water her plants.

Website: MBaileyart.com